Down by the Station

BY WILL HILLENBRAND

WITHDRAWN

RAIL ROAD CROSSING

Voyager Books · Harcourt, Inc.

SAN DIEGO   NEW YORK   LONDON

First Voyager Books edition 2002
Voyager Books is a trademark of Harcourt, Inc., registered in the United States of America and/or other jurisdictions.

The Library of Congress has cataloged the hardcover edition as follows:
Hillenbrand, Will.
Down by the station/by Will Hillenbrand.
p. cm.
Summary: In this version of a familiar song, baby animals ride to the children's zoo on the zoo train.
1. Children's songs—Texts. [1. Zoo animals—Songs and music. 2. Animals—Infancy—Songs and music. 3. Songs.]
I. Title.
PZ8.3.H553Do 1999
782.42—dc21
[E]   98-41770
ISBN 978-0-15-201804-7
ISBN 978-0-15-216790-5 pb

SCP   25 24 23 22 21 20 19

4500701510

The illustrations in this book were created in mixed media on vellum, painted on both sides.
The display type was set in Belwe Bold Condensed.
The text type was set in Worcester Round Bold.
Color separations by Bright Arts Ltd., Hong Kong
Printed in China by RR Donnelley
Production supervision by Sandra Grebenar and Wendi Taylor
Designed by Kaelin Chappell and Will Hillenbrand

Printed in China

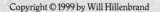

To Liz; Charlie;
my wife, Jane;
and my son, Ian

Down by the station
early in the morning.

See the little puffer-bellies
all in a row.

See the engine driver
pull his little lever. . . .

Puff, puff,
Toot, toot,
Off we go!

Down by the elephants
early in the morning.
See the little calf
waiting to go.
See the engine driver
pull his little lever. . . .

Puff, puff,
Toot, toot,
Thrump, thrump,
Off we go!

Down by the flamingos
early in the morning.
See the little chick
waiting to go.
See the engine driver
pull his little lever. . . .

Puff, puff,
Toot, toot,
Thrump, thrump,
Peep, peep,
Off we go!

Down by the pandas
early in the morning.
See the little cub
waiting to go.
See the engine driver
pull his little lever. . . .

Puff, puff,
Toot, toot,
Thrump, thrump,
Peep, peep,
Grump, grump,
Off we go!

Down by the tigers
early in the morning.
See the little cub
waiting to go.
See the engine driver
pull his little lever. . . .

Puff, puff,
Toot, toot,
Thrump, thrump,
Peep, peep,
Grump, grump,
Mew, mew,
Off we go!

Down by the seals
early in the morning.
See the little pup
waiting to go.
See the engine driver
pull his little lever. . . .

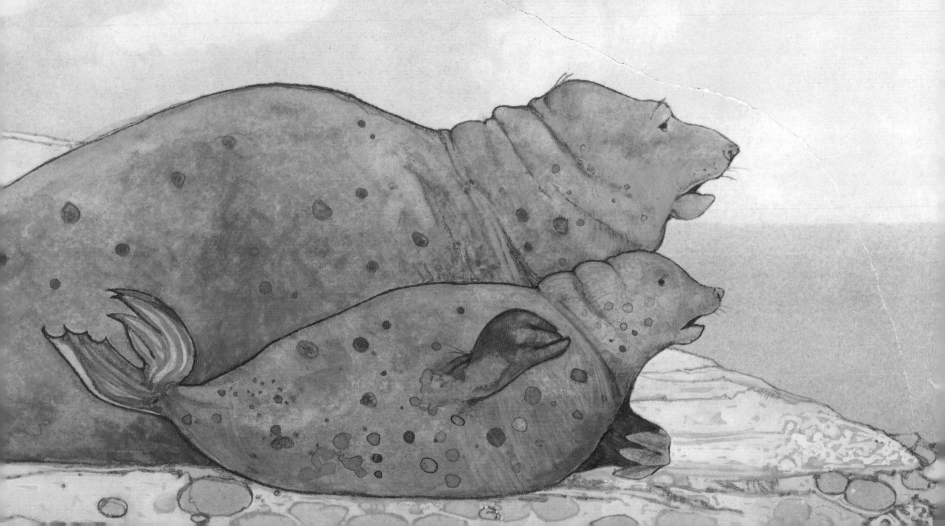

Puff, puff,
Toot, toot,
Thrump, thrump,
Peep, peep,
Grump, grump,
Mew, mew,
Flip, flop . . .

Uh-oh!

Phew!

Down by the kangaroos
early in the morning.
See the little joey
waiting to go.

See the engine driver
pull his little lever. . . .

Puff, puff,
Toot, toot,
Thrump, thrump,
Peep, peep,
Grump, grump,
Mew, mew,
Flip, flop,
Bump, bump,
Off we go!

Down by the children's zoo
early in the morning.
See the baby animals
exit in a row.
See the engine driver
pull his little lever. . . .

Puff, puff,
Toot, toot . . .

Off we go!

Down by the Station

Down by the sta - tion ear - ly in the morn - ing,

See the lit - tle puf - fer - bel - lies all in a row.

See the en - gine driv - er pull his lit - tle lev - er.

Puff, puff, Toot, toot, Off we go!